BELWIN

CLARINET METHOD

(IN THREE VOLUMES)

By

KENNETH GEKELER

EDITED BY

NILO W. HOVEY

BOOK
TWO

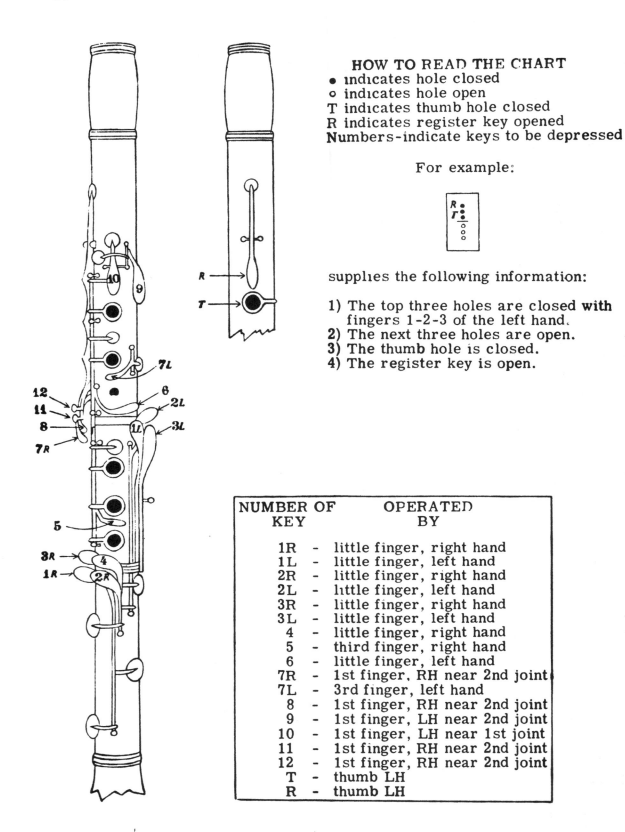

HOW TO READ THE CHART

● indicates hole closed
○ indicates hole open
T indicates thumb hole closed
R indicates register key opened
Numbers - indicate keys to be depressed

For example:

supplies the following information:

1) The top three holes are closed **with** fingers 1-2-3 of the left hand.
2) The next three holes are open.
3) The thumb hole is closed.
4) The register key is open.

NUMBER OF KEY		OPERATED BY
1R	-	little finger, right hand
1L	-	little finger, left hand
2R	-	little finger, right hand
2L	-	little finger, left hand
3R	-	little finger, right hand
3L	-	little finger, left hand
4	-	little finger, right hand
5	-	third finger, right hand
6	-	little finger, left hand
7R	-	1st finger, RH near 2nd joint
7L	-	3rd finger, left hand
8	-	1st finger, RH near 2nd joint
9	-	1st finger, LH near 2nd joint
10	-	1st finger, LH near 1st joint
11	-	1st finger, RH near 2nd joint
12	-	1st finger, RH near 2nd joint
T	-	thumb LH
R	-	thumb LH

EL 322-31

FINGERING CHART

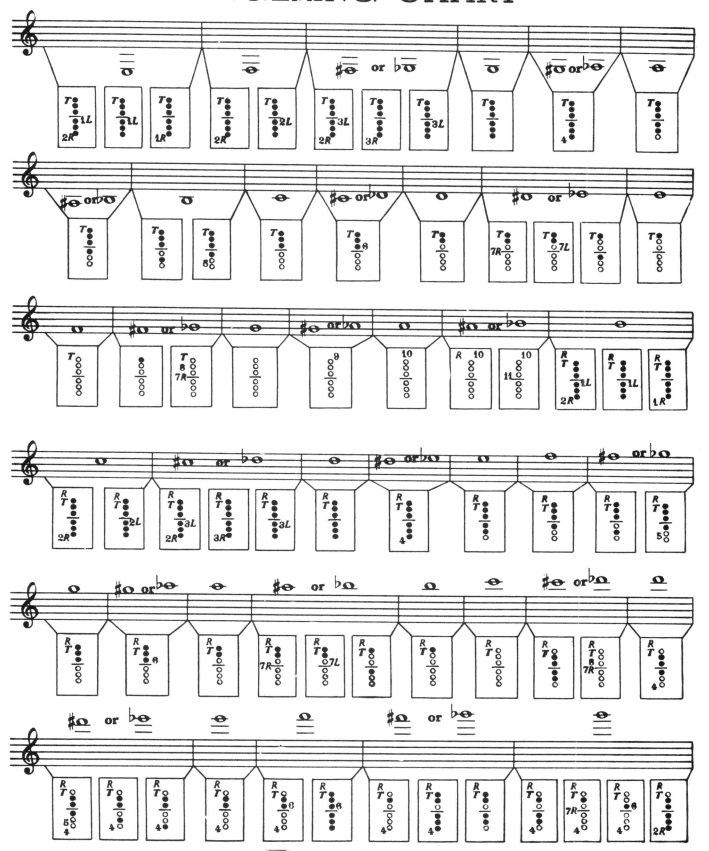

A thorough knowledge of the key signatures and rhythms of pages 40, 41 and 42 should be required of the student who is continuing in Book II. If lack of facility in any key or rhythmic pattern is evident, that portion should be reviewed frequently as progress continues.

Review of Keys

Note: The letters "R" and "L" are used as abbreviations for "right" and "left". A note marked "R" should be taken on the right hand and one marked "L" should be taken on the left hand. Such symbols are used as reminders for fingerings already introduced.

Review of Keys

*(1)
A new important fin-
gering for high B♭.

*(2)
A new note, high E:

EL 322

Review of Rhythms

This page will serve as a test of the student's ability to COUNT and PLAY the rhythmic figures introduced in Book I.

The Chromatic Scale

The sketch below, a facsimile of a piano keyboard, may be employed to good advantage in explaining the chromatic scale and enharmonics.

Two tones of the same pitch but identified by different letter names, (F♯ and G♭ for example) are known as "enharmonics". Thus, C♯ is the "enharmonic" of D♭, D♯ of E♭, G♯ of A♭, A♯ of B♭. Locate these tones on the keyboard and verify the above facts.

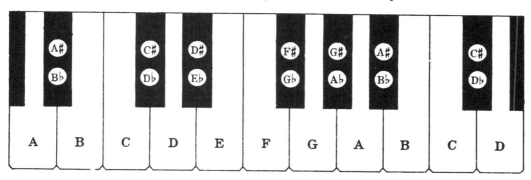

IMPORTANT: Strict adherance to correct fingerings should be emphasized. Particular attention should be paid to the following notes for which a different fingering has been used in scale-wise motion.

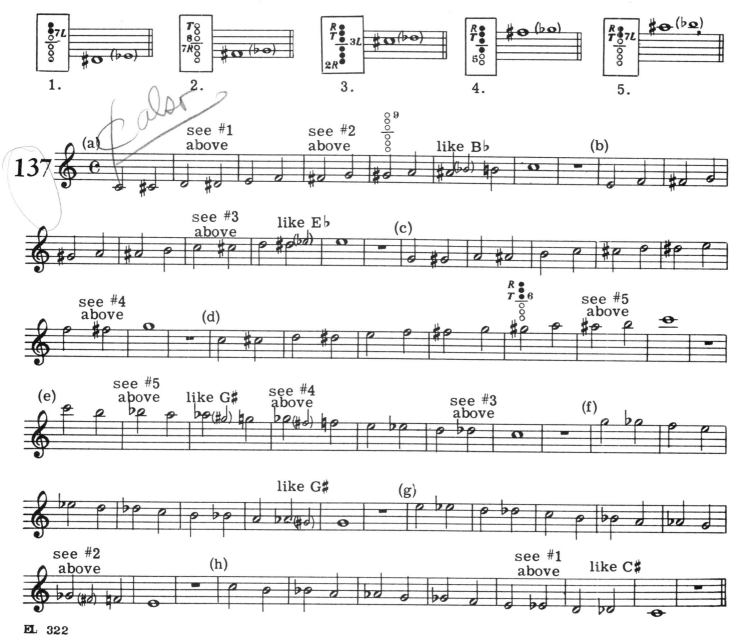

Alla Breve

o = two beats; ♩ = one beat; ♪ = one-half beat

DUET

Additional assignment: Play the chromatic exercise 137 in alla breve (¢).

Alla Breve

Note: A dot placed over or under a note signifies that the note shall be played "staccato". (separated, detached)

DUET

Additional assignment: Memorize section (a) of the chromatic scale (exercise 137).

EL 322

Alla Breve

Additional assignment: Memorize section (d) of the chromatic scale (exercise 137) in ¢.

Alla Breve

Additional assignment: Play the chromatic scale 2 octaves (ascending) from memory. (¢).

EL 322

The Key of A Major

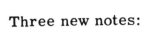
Three new notes: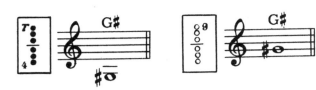

MECHANISM

151

Avoid excessive finger motion.

Note: Low G♯ can be taken ONLY on the RIGHT HAND. Therefore any preceding or following note involving the use of keys 1, 2 or 3 must be taken on the LEFT HAND.

152

A SCALE EXERCISE
(3rds and the Major arpeggio on page 65)

153

THE A SCALE FOR MEMORIZATION

154

*After completing this page, play six major scales and the chromatic (ascending) from memory.

Three-Eight Meter

♪ = one beat   ♩ = two beats   ♩. = three beats

Common rhythmic figures

Additional assignment: Memorize section (e) of exercise 137 (¢) and review exercise 153.

Six Eight Meter

Additional assignment: Memorize section (h) of exercise 137 (¢).

Six Eight Meter

Additional assignment: Play the chromatic scale two octaves (ascending and descending) from memory. (see exercise 164)

EL 322

Chromatic

Spend a few minutes on some chromatic exercise every day!

Extending the Register

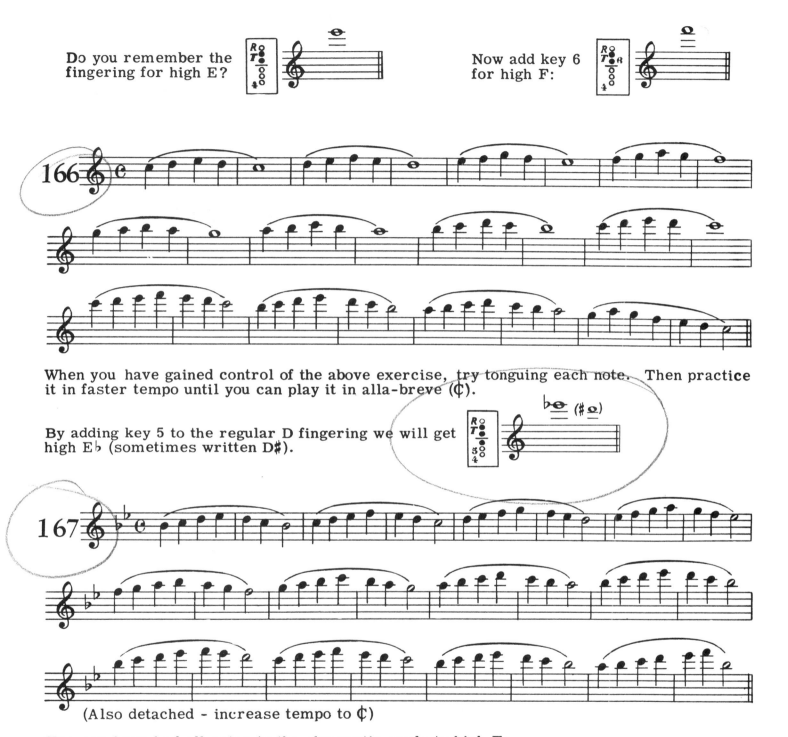

Do you remember the fingering for high E?

Now add key 6 for high F:

When you have gained control of the above exercise, try tonguing each note. Then practice it in faster tempo until you can play it in alla-breve (¢).

By adding key 5 to the regular D fingering we will get high E♭ (sometimes written D♯).

(Also detached - increase tempo to ¢)

You now have had all notes in the chromatic scale to high F:

like E♭   like C♯

Note: If the instructor wishes to use the 3-octave chromatic scale at this time it may be found on page 65. Eighth notes may be substituted for the sixteenths.

EL 322

The Key of E♭ Major

Three new notes:

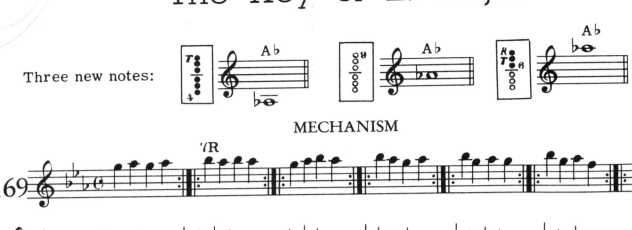

MECHANISM

169

Note: Low A♭ can be taken ONLY on the RIGHT HAND. Therefore any preceding or following note involving the use of keys 1, 2 or 3 must be taken on the LEFT HAND.

170

A SCALE EXERCISE
(3rds and the Major arpeggio on page 65)

171

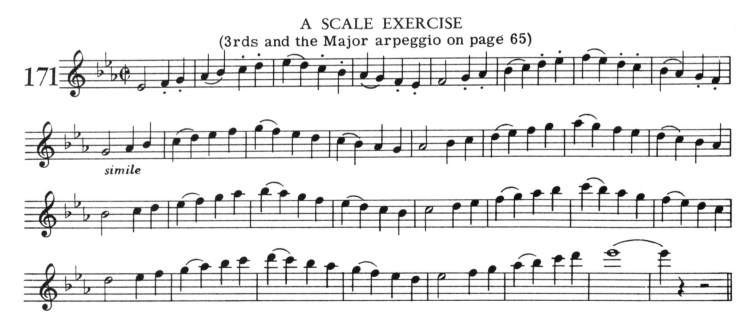

simile

THE E♭ SCALE FOR MEMORIZATION

172

* After completing this page, play seven major scales and the chromatic from memory.

Triplets

With three notes of equal value to the beat

DUET

(Review 171)

Six-Eight Meter

(in two beats)

Compare
these
Rhythms

175

176

177

Try exercise 165 in fast six-eight. (two beats to the measure).

Six-Eight Meter

(in two beats)

Try exercises 158 and 159 in fast six-eight. (two beats to the measure.)

EL 322

Six-Eight Meter

(in two beats)

Compare these rhythms:

Try exercises 160 and 161 in fast six-eight. (two beats to the measure.)

Six-Eight Meter

(in two beats)

The following familiar melodies have been selected as excellent examples of the "march type" of six-eight meter.

WHEN JOHNNY COMES MARCHING HOME

*The above are good examples of the fingering for high B♭

Try the duet (exercise 162) in fast six-eight. (two beats to the measure).

EL 322

Syncopation

Sixteenth Notes

Repeat these measures many times. Start with four slow beats and increase the speed gradually until you can play each one with two beats.

Sixteenth Notes

First tongue each note. Then articulate as written.

Sixteenth Notes

Note: Following the above pattern, try the other scales you have memorized.

64

Sixteenth Notes

198 Play the A scale 2 octaves using this rhythm pattern:

199 Play the Eb scale 2 octaves using this rhythm pattern:

MIXED RHYTHMS

200

201 Play the D scale 2 octaves using this rhythm pattern·

202

Chromatic

1st - Play the exercise several times as written.
2nd - After you have attained reasonably good control, try omitting all dotted half-notes except the high F and the final note.
3rd - When you have sufficient technical skill and control of the breath, omit all dotted half-notes except the last.

THIRDS AND ARPEGGIOS
in A and E♭

* Use [R T] for high B♭.

The Dotted Eighth and Sixteenth

Compare these rhythms:

The first two notes are equal:

The first note is <u>twice</u> as long as the second:

The first note is <u>three</u> times as long as the second:

In SLOW TEMPO give full value to each note and visualize four sixteenths as you play:

In FAST TEMPO give a little more stress to the dotted eighth. Play the sixteenth short, light and very close to the following note:

THEME FROM THE NEW WORLD SYMPHONY

The Dotted Eighth and Sixteenth

VARIATION ON A THEME

208

Con grazia

* What is the correct fingering for the notes so marked?

DUET

209

Allegretto

The Dotted Eighth and Sixteenth

A GRAND MARCH

THEME FROM "CORONATION MARCH"

Meyerbeer

A RIDDLE IN RHYTHM

Reasonable facility in seven major keys and chromatic, and the ability to count and play the the rhythmic figures contained in this book should be considered pre-requisites to Book III.